William Strachan

**Dramatic Selections from Noted Poets**

William Strachan

**Dramatic Selections from Noted Poets**

ISBN/EAN: 9783337342425

Printed in Europe, USA, Canada, Australia, Japan

Cover: Foto ©Andreas Hilbeck / pixelio.de

More available books at **www.hansebooks.com**

# DRAMATIC SELECTIONS

—FROM—

# NOTED * POETS:

Shakespeare, Burns,
Thos. Campbell, Sir Walter Scott,
Bryant, Eugene Hall,

—AND—

# OTHER FAMOUS AUTHORS.

COMPILED BY
## WILLIAM STRACHAN,
A GRADUATE OF THE MINE,—AND RECITED BY HIM.

## PRICE 25 CENTS.

SALEM, OHIO:
THE THOS. J. WALTON STEAM PRINTING HOUSE.
1892.

# PREFACE.

THIS little pamphlet is respectfully dedicated to the lovers and patrons of the POETICAL, and has been carefully compiled by the author, with the belief that there are many admirers of the POETS in this broad land, who will gladly welcome such a volume. With feelings of reluctance he has undertaken this work, knowing how inadequate he is to perform the task, yet hoping for an indulgent support of the public, when it is understood it has been done by one who has never had the advantages of a collegiate or even high school education—still, thinking that some merit may be found in the selections made, and buoyed up with the hope that they will meet with favor from an impartial public, he launches them forth, trusting that they may meet with favorable reception—yet believing they will not fill the belly, or clothe the back, or keep the wolf from the door—still he has faith they will help to make the blood circulate, and expand the arterial current, and greatly strengthen the nerve tension.

With the hope that the political kettle will not put out the poetical fire, believing that both are necessary for the interests of all, the author holds that memory is dear to every one, and that the selections herein made can be readily committed to memory, and when once learned will be long retained.

The following are the conditions and terms on which this issue is sent forth:—In any locality, village, hamlet, town or city, where one hundred persons subscribe, and each take one copy at the advertised price, he will come to the place and recite any three pieces from the collection, from memory—admitting those only who are purchasers of the pamphlet. But subscribers must furnish the house and all necessary accommodations for the entertainment.

Humbly,

THE COMPILER.

Entered, according to act of Congress, in the year 1892, by WILLIAM STRACHAN, In the office of the Librarian of Congress, Washington, D. C.

# DRAMATIC SELECTIONS.

———✳———

## THE LADY OF THE LAKE.

SIR WALTER SCOTT.

### CANTO FIFTH.—THE COMBAT.

FAIR as the earliest beam of eastern light,
  When first by the bewilder'd pilgrim spied,
It smiles upon the dreary brow of night,
  And silvers o'er the torrent's flowing tide,
And lights the fearful path on mountain side,
  Fair as that beam, although the fairest far,
Giving to horror grace, to danger pride,
  Shine martial Faith, and Courtesy's bright star,
Through all the wreckful storms that cloud the brow of War.

That early beam, so fair and sheen,
Was twinkling through the hazel screen,
When, rousing at its glimmer red,
The warriors left their lowly bed,
Look'd out upon the dappled sky,
Mutter'd their soldier matins by,
And then awaked their fire, to steal,
As short and rude, their soldier meal.
That o'er, the Gael around him threw
His graceful plaid of varied hue,
And, true to promise, led the way,
By thicket green and mountain gray.
A wildering path!—they winded now
Along the precipice's brow,
Commanding the rich scenes beneath,
The windings of the Forth and Teith,
And all the vales beneath that lie,
Till Stirling's turrets melt in sky;
Then, sunk in copse, their farthest glance,
Gain'd not the length of horseman's lance.

'Twas oft so steep, the foot was fain
Assistance from the hand to gain;
So tangled oft, that, bursting through,
Each hawthorn shed her showers of dew,—
That diamond dew, so pure and clear,
It rivals all but Beauty's tear!

At length they came where, stern and steep,
The hill sinks down upon the deep,
Here Venuachar in silver flows,
There, ridge on ridge, Benledi rose;
Ever the hollow path twined on,
Beneath steep bank and threatening stone;
An hundred men might hold the post
With hardihood against a host.
The rugged mountain's scanty cloak
Was dwarfish shrubs of birch and oak,
With shingles bare, and cliffs between,
And patches bright of bracken green,
And heather black, that waved so high,
It held the copse in rivalry.
But where the lake slept deep and still,
Dank oziers fringed the swamp and hill,
And oft both path and hill were torn,
Where wintry torrents down had borne,
And heap'd upon the cumber'd land
Its wreck of gravel, rocks, and sand.
So toilsome was the road to trace,
The guide, abating of his pace,
Led slowly through the pass's jaws,
And ask'd Fitz-James by what strange cause
He sought these wilds? traversed by few,
Without a pass from Roderick Dhu.

" Brave Gael, my pass in danger tried,
Hangs in my belt and by my side;
Yet, sooth to tell," the Saxon said,
"I dreamt not now to claim its aid.
When here, but three days since, I came,
Bewildered in pursuit of game,
All seem'd as peaceful and as still
As the mist slumbering on yon hill;

Thy dangerous Chief was then afar,
Nor soon expected back from war.
Thus said, at least, my mountain guide,
Though deep, perchance, the villain lied."—
" Yet why a second venture try?"
" A warrior thou, and ask me why!—
Moves our free course by such fix'd cause,
As gives the poor mechanic laws:
Enough, I sought to drive away
The lazy hours of peaceful day:
Slight cause will then suffice to guide,
A Knight's free footsteps far and wide—
A falcon flown, a greyhound stray'd,
The merry glance of mountain maid:
Or, if a path be dangerous known,
The danger's self is lure alone."

"Thy secret keep, I urge thee not:—
Yet, ere again ye sought this spot,
Say, heard ye nought of Lowland war,
Against Clan-Alpine, raised by Mar?"
—"No, by my word;—of bands prepared
To guard King James's sports I heard;
Nor doubt I aught, but, when they hear
This muster of the mountaineer,
Their pennons will abroad be flung,
Which else in Doune had peaceful hung."—
" Free be they flung!—for we are loth
Their silken folds should feast the moth.
Free be they flung!—as free shall wave
Clan-Alpine's pine in banner brave.
But, Stranger, peaceful since you came,
Bewilder'd in the mountain game,
Whence the bold boast by which you show
Vich-Alpine's vow'd and mortal foe?"—
" Warrior, but yester-morn I knew
Nought of thy Chieftain, Roderick Dhu,
Save as an outlawed desperate man,
The chief of a rebellious clan,
Who, in the Regent's court and sight,
With ruffian dagger stabb'd a knight;

Yet this alone might from his part
Sever each true and loyal heart."

Wrathful at such arraignment foul,
Dark lower'd the clansman's sable scowl;
A space he paused, then sternly said,
"And heard'st thou why he drew his blade?
Heard'st thou that shameful word and blow
Brought Roderick's vengeance on his foe?
What reck'd the Chieftain if he stood
On Highland heath, or Holy-Rood?
He rights such wrong where it is given,
If it were in the court of heaven."—
"Still was it outrage;—yet, 'tis true,
Not then claim'd sovereignty his due;
While Albany, with feeble hand,
Held borrow'd truncheon of command,
The young King, mew'd in Stirling tower,
Was stranger to respect and power.
But then, thy Chieftain's robber life!—
Winning mean prey by causeless strife,
Wrenching from ruined Lowland swain
His herds and harvests rear'd in vain.—
Methinks a soul like thine should scorn
The spoils from such foul foray borne."
The Gael beheld him grim the while,
And answer'd with disdainful smile,—
"Saxon, from yonder mountain high,
I mark'd thee send delighted eye,
Far to the south and east, where lay,
Extended in succession gay,
Deep waving fields and pastures green,
With gentle slopes and groves between:—
These fertile plains, that soften'd vale,
Were once the birthright of the Gael;
The stranger came with iron hand,
And from our fathers reft the land.
Where dwell we now? See, rudely swell
Crag over crag, and fell o'er fell.
Ask we this savage hill we tread,
For fatten'd steer or household bread;

Ask we for flocks these shingles dry,
And well the mountain might reply,—
'To you, as to your sires of yore,
Belong the target and claymore!
I give you shelter in my breast,
Your own good blades must win the rest.'
Pent in this fortress of the North,
Think'st thou we will not sally forth,
To spoil the spoiler as we may,
And from the robber rend the prey?
Ay, by my soul!—While on yon plain
The Saxon rears one shock of grain;
While, of ten thousand herds, there strays
But one along yon river's maze,—
The Gael, of plain and river heir,
Shall, with strong hand, redeem his share.
Where live the mountain chiefs who hold,
That plundering Lowland field and fold
Is aught but retribution true?
Seek other cause 'gainst Roderick Dhu."—

Answer'd Fitz-James,—"And, if I sought,
Think'st thou no other could be brought?
What deem ye of my path waylaid?
My life given o'er to ambuscade?"—
"As of a meed to rashness due:
Hadst thou sent warning fair and true,—
I seek my hound, or falcon stray'd,
I seek, good faith, a Highland maid,—
Free hadst thou been to come and go;
But secret path marks secret foe.
Nor yet, for this, even as a spy,
Hadst thou, unheard, been doom'd to die,
Save to fulfill an augury."—
"Well, let it pass; nor will I now
Fresh cause of enmity avow,
To chafe thy mood and cloud thy brow.
Enough, I am by promise tied
To match me with this man of pride;
Twice have I sought Clan-Alpine's glen
In peace; but when I come agen

I come with banner, brand, and bow,
As leader seeks his mortal foe.
For love-lorn swain, in lady's bower,
Ne'er panted for the appointed hour,
As I, until before me stand
This rebel Chieftain and his band!"—

"Have, then, thy wish!"—He whistled shrill,
And he was answered from the hill;
Wild as the scream of the curlew,
From crag to crag the signal flew.
Instant, through copse and heath, arose
Bonnets and spears and bended bows;
On right, on left, above, below,
Sprung up at once the lurking foe;
From shingles gray their lances start,
The bracken bush sends forth the dart,
The rushes and the willow-wand
Are bristling into axe and brand,
And every tuft of broom gives life
To plaided warrior armed for strife.
That whistle garrison'd the glen
At once with full five hundred men,
As if the yawning hill to heaven
A subterranean host had given.
Watching their leader's beck and will,
All silent there they stood, and still.
Like the loose crags, whose threatening mass
Lay tottering o'er the hollow pass,
As if an infant's touch could urge
Their headlong passage down the verge,
With step and weapon forward flung,
Upon the mountain-side they hung.
The Mountaineer cast glance of pride
Along Benledi's living side,
Then fix'd his eyes and sable brow
Full on Fitz-James—"How say'st thou now?
These are Clan-Alpine's warriors true,
And, Saxon,—I am Roderick Dhu!"

Fitz-James was brave:—Though to his heart
The life-blood thrilled with sudden start,

He mann'd himself with dauntless air,
Returned the chief his haughty stare;
His back against a rock he bore,
And firmly placed his foot before:—
"Come one, come all! this rock shall fly
From its firm base as soon as I."
Sir Roderick mark'd—and in his eyes
Respect was mingled with surprise,
And the stern joy which warriors feel
In foemen worthy of their steel.
Short space he stood—then waved his hand:
Down sunk the disappearing band;
Each warrior vanish'd where he stood,
In broom or bracken, heath or wood;
Sunk brand and spear and bended bow,
In oziers pale and copses low;
It seemed as if their mother Earth
Had swallow'd up her warlike birth.
The wind's last breath had toss'd in air,
Pennon, and plaid, and plumage fair,—
The next but swept a lone hill-side,
Where heath and fern were waving wide:
The sun's last glance was glinted back
From spear and glaive, from targe and jack,
The next, all unreflected, shone
On bracken green, and cold gray stone.

Fitz-James looked round—yet scarce believed
The witness that his sight received;
Such apparition well might seem
Delusion of a dreadful dream.
Sir Roderick in suspense he eyed,
And to his look the Chief replied,
"Fear nought—nay, that I need not say—
But—doubt not aught from mine array,
Thou art my guest;—I pledged my word
As far as Coilantogle ford:
Nor would I call a clansman's brand
For aid against one valiant hand,
Though on our strife lay every vale
Rent by the Saxon from the Gael.

So move we on;—I only meant
To show the reed on which you leant,
Deeming this pass you might pursue
Without a pass from Roderick Dhu."
They moved:—I said Fitz-James was brave,
As ever knight that belted glaive;
Yet dare not say, that now his blood
Kept on its wont and temper'd flood,
As, following Roderick's stride, he drew
That seeming lonesome pathway through,
Which yet, by fearful proof, was rife
With lances, that, to take his life,
Waited but signal from a guide,
So late dishonor'd and defied.
Ever, by stealth, his eye sought round
The vanished guardians of the ground,
And still, from copse and heather deep,
Fancy saw spear and broadsword peep,
And in the plover's shrilly strain,
The signal whistle heard again.
Nor breathed he free till far behind
The pass was left; for then they wind
Along a wide and level green,
Where neither tree nor tuft was seen,
Nor rush, nor bush of broom was near,
To hide a bonnet or a spear.

The Chief in silence strode before,
And reach'd that torrent's sounding shore,
Which, daughter of three mighty lakes,
From Vennachar in silver breaks,
Sweeps through the plain and ceaseless mines
On Bochastle the mouldering lines,
Where Rome, the Empress of the world,
Of yore her eagle wings unfurl'd.
And here his course the Chieftain staid,
Threw down his target and his plaid,
And to the Lowland warrior said:—
"Bold Saxon! to his promise just,
Vich-Alpine has discharged his trust.
This murderous Chief, this ruthless man,

This head of a rebellious clan,
Hath led thee safe through watch and ward,
Far past Clan-Alpine's outmost guard.
Now, man to man, and steel to steel,
A chieftain's vengeance thou shalt feel.
See, here all vantageless I stand,
Armed, like thyself, with single brand:
For this is Coilantogle ford,
And thou must keep thee with thy sword."

The Saxon paused:—"I ne'er delay'd
When foeman bade me draw my blade;
Nay, more, brave Chief, I vowed thy death:
Yet sure thy fair and generous faith,
And my deep debt for life preserved,
A better meed have well deserved:
Can nought but blood our feud atone?
Are there no means?"—"No, stranger, none!
And hear,—to fire thy flagging zeal,—
The Saxon cause rests on thy steel;
For thus spoke Fate, by prophet bred
Between the living and the dead:
'Who spills the foremost foeman's life,
His party conquers in the strife.' "—
"Then, by my word," the Saxon said,
"The riddle is already read.
Seek yonder brake beneath the cliff,—
There lies Red Murdoch, stark and still.
Thus Fate has solved her prophecy,
Then yield to Fate, and not to me.
To James, at Stirling, let us go,
When, if thou wilt be still his foe,
Or if the King shall not agree
To grant thee grace and favor free,
I plight mine honor, oath, and word,
That, to thy native strengths restored,
With each advantage shalt thou stand,
That aids thee now to guard thy land."

Dark lightning flash'd from Roderick's eye—
"Soars thy presumption, then, so high,
Because a wretched kern ye slew,

Homage to name to Roderick Dhu?
He yields not, he, to man nor Fate!
Thou add'st but fuel to my hate:—
My clansman's blood demands revenge.
Not yet prepared?—By heaven, I change
My thought, and hold thy valor light
As that of some vain carpet-knight,
Who ill deserved my courteous care,
And whose best boast is but to wear
A braid of his fair lady's hair.''—
" I thank thee, Roderick, for the word!
It nerves my heart, it steels my sword;
For I have sworn this braid to stain
In the best blood that warms thy vein.
Now, truce, farewell! and, ruth, begone!—
Yet think not that by thee alone,
Proud Chief! can courtesy be shown!
Though not from copse, or heath, or cairn,
Start at my whistle clansmen stern,
Of this small horn one feeble blast
Would fearful odds against thee cast.
But fear not—doubt not—which thou wilt,
We try this quarrel hilt to hilt.''
Then each at once his falchion drew,
Each on the ground his scabbard threw,
Each look'd to sun, to stream, and plain,
As what they ne'er might see again;
Then foot, and point, and eye opposed,
In dubious strife they darkly closed.

Ill fared it then with Roderick Dhu,
That on the field his targe he threw,
Whose brazen studs and tough bull-hide
Had death so often dashed aside;
For, train'd abroad his arms to wield,
Fitz-James's blade was sword and shield.
He practised every pass and ward,
To thrust, to strike, to feint, to guard;
While less expert, though stronger far,
The Gael maintain'd unequal war.
Three times in closing strife they stood,

And thrice the Saxon blade drank blood;
No stinted draught, no scanty tide,
The gushing flood the tartans dyed.
Fierce Roderick felt the fatal drain,
And shower'd his blows like wintry rain;
And, as firm rock or castle-roof,
Against the winter shower is proof,
The foe, invulnerable still,
Foil'd his wile rage by steady skill:
Till, at advantage ta'en his brand
Forced Roderick's weapon from his hand,
And backward borne upon the lea,
Brought the proud chieftain to his knee.
"Now yield thee, or by Him who made
The world, thy heart's blood dyes my blade!"
"Thy threats, thy mercy, I defy!
Let recreant yield, who fears to die."
—Like adder darting from his coil,
Like wolf that dashes through the toil,
Like mountain-cat who guards her young,
Full at Fitz-James's throat he sprung;
Received, but reck'd not of a wound,
And lock'd his arms his foeman round.—
Now, gallant Saxon, hold thine own!
No maiden's hand is round thee thrown!
That desperate grasp thy frame might feel,
Through bars of brass and triple steel!—
They tug, they strain, down, down they go,
The Gael above, Fitz-James below:
The Chieftain's gripe his throat compress'd,
His knee was planted on his breast;
His clotted locks he backward threw,
Across his brow his hand he drew,
From blood and mist to clear his sight,
Then gleam'd aloft his dagger bright!—
—But hate and fury ill supplied
The stream of life's exhausted tide,
And all too late the advantage came,
To turn the odds of deadly game;
For, while the dagger gleam'd on high,
Reel'd soul and sense, reel'd brain and eye,

Down came the blow! but in the heath
The erring blade found bloodless sheath.
The struggling foe may now unclasp
The fainting Chief's relaxing grasp;
Unwounded from the dreadful close,
But breathless all, Fitz-James arose.

He falter'd thanks to Heaven for life,
Redeem'd, unhoped, from desperate strife.

## TANTALLON CASTLE.

### WALTER SCOTT.

Not far advanced was morning day,
When Marmion did his troop array,
    To Surrey's Camp to ride;
He had safe conduct for his band,
Beneath the royal seal and hand,
    And Douglas gave a guide.

The ancient Earl, with stately grace
Would Clara on her palfrey place,
But whispered in an undertone,
Let the hawk stoop, his prey has flown.
The train from out the Castle drew,
But Marmion stopp'd to bid adieu:
   "Tho' something I might 'plain" he said,
"Of cold respect to stranger guest,
Sent hither by the king's behest,
While in Tantallon's Towers I staid,
Part we in friendship from your land,
And, noble Earl, receive my hand."
But Douglas round him drew his cloak,
Folded his arms, and thus he spoke,
"My manors, halls and towers shall still
Be open at my sovereign's will,
To each one whom he lists, howe'er
Unmeet to be the owner's peer.
My castles are my king's alone,
From turret to foundation stone,

The hand of Douglas is his own,
And never shall, in friendly grasp,
The hand of such as Marmion clasp.''

Burned Marmion's swarthy cheek like fire,
And shook his very frame for ire,
"And this to me," he said,
"And 'twere not for thy hoary beard,
Such hand as Marmion had not spared,
To cleave the Douglas head!
And first, I tell thee, haughty peer,
He who does England's message here,
Although the meanest in her State,
May well, proud Angus, be thy mate.
And Douglas, more, I tell thee here,
Even in thy pitch of pride,
Here, in thy hold, thy vassals near,
I tell thee, thou'rt defied!
And if thou said'st I am not peer
To any lord in Scotland here,
Lowland or Highland, far or near,
Lord Angus, *thou—hast—lied!''*

On the Earl's cheek, the flush of rage
O'ercame the ashen hue of age ;
Fierce he broke forth; "And, darest thou then
To beard the lion in his den,
The Douglas in his hall?
And hop'st thou thence unscath'd to go?
*No,* by St. Bryde of Bothwell, *no!*
Up drawbridge, grooms—what, warder, ho!
Let the portcullis fall.''
Lord Marmion turned, well was his need,
And dashed the rowels in his steed,
Like arrow through the arch-way sprung;
The ponderous gate behind him rung,
To pass, there was such scanty room,
The bars descending, grazed his plume.

The steed along the drawbridge flies,
Just as it trembled on the rise:
Not lighter does the swallow skim

Along the smooth lake's level brim;
And when Lord Marmion reached his band
He halts and turns with clinched hand,
And shout of loud defiance pours,
And shook his gauntlet at the towers.
"*Horse! horse!*" the Douglas cried,"*and chase!*"
But soon he rein'd his fury's pace:
"A royal messenger he came,
Though most unworthy of the name:
Saint Mary, mend my fiery mood!
Old age ne'er cools the Douglas' blood;
I thought to slay him where he stood.
'T is pity of him too," he cried:
"Bold he can speak, and fairly ride;
I warrant him a warrior tried."
With this, his mandate he recalls,
And slowly seeks his castle walls.

## THE DOWNFALL OF POLAND.

### THOMAS CAMPBELL.

Oh! sacred Truth! thy triumph ceas'd awhile,
And Hope, thy sister, ceased with thee to smile,
When leagu'd oppression pour'd to northern wars
Her whisker'd pandoors and her fierce hussars,
Wav'd her dread standard to the breeze of morn,
Peal'd her loud drum, and twang'd her trumpet horn;
Tumultuous horror brooded o'er her van,
Presaging wrath to Poland,—and to man!

Warsaw's last champion from her hights surveyed,
Wide o'er the fields, a waste of ruin laid;
"Oh! heaven!" he cried, "my bleeding country save,
Is there no hand on high to shield the brave?
Yet, though destruction sweep those lovely plains,
Rise! fellow-men! *our country* yet remains!
By that dread name we wave the sword on high,
And swear *for her to live—with her to die!*"

He said, and on the rampart-hights array'd

His trusty warriors, few, but undismay'd;
Firm-pac'd and slow, a horrid front they form,
Still as the breeze, but dreadful as the storm;
Low murmuring sounds along their banners fly,
*Revenge or death*—the watch-word and reply;
Then peal'd the notes, omnipotent to charm,
And the loud tocsin toll'd their last alarm.

In vain, alas! in vain, ye gallant few!
From rank to rank, your volley'd thunder flew!
Oh bloodiest picture in the book of time,
Sarmatia fell, unwept, without a crime;
Found not a generous friend, a pitying foe,
Strength in her arms, nor mercy in her woe!
Dropp'd from her nerveless grasp the shatter'd spear,
Clos'd her bright eye, and curb'd her high career;
Hope, for a season, bade the world farewell,
And freedom shriek'd—as Kosciusko fell!

The sun went down, nor ceas'd the carnage there,
Tumultuous murder shook the midnight air;
On Prague's proud arch the fires of ruin glow,
His blood-dyed waters murmuring far below;
The storm prevails, the rampart yields away,
Bursts the wild cry of horror and dismay!
Hark! as the smoldering piles with thunder fall,
A thousand shrieks for hopeless mercy call!
Earth shook, red meteors flash'd along the sky,
And conscious Nature shudder'd at the cry!

Oh righteous heaven! ere Freedom found a grave,
Why slept the sword, omnipotent to save?
Where was *thine* arm, O Vengeance! where thy rod,
That smote the foes of Zion and of God?
That crushed proud Ammon, when his iron car
Was yoke'd in wrath, and thunder'd from afar?
Where was the storm that slumber'd till the host
Of blood-stain'd Pharaoh left their trembling coast;
Then, bade the deep in wild commotion flow,
And heav'd an ocean on their march below?

Departed spirits of the mighty dead!

Ye that at Marathon and Leuctra bled!
Friends of the world! restore your swords to man,
Fight in his sacred cause and lead the van!
Yet, for Sarmatia's tears of blood atone,
And make her arm puissant as your own!
Oh! once again to Freedom's cause return
The patriot TELL—the BRUCE OF BANNOCKBURN!

## LOCHIEL'S WARNING.

### THOMAS CAMPBELL.

#### WIZARD.

Lochiel, Lochiel, beware of the day,
When the Lowlands shall meet thee in battle array;
For a field of the dead rushes red on my sight,
And the clans of Culloden are scattered in fight;
They rally, they bleed, for their kingdom and crown,
Woe, woe, to the riders that trample them down,
Proud Cumberland prances, insulting the slain,
And their hoof-beaten bosoms are trod to the plain.
But hark! through the fast flashing lightning of war,
What steed to the desert flies frantic and far.
'T is thine, oh Glenullin, whose bride shall await,
Like a love lighted watchfire all night at the gate,
A steed comes at morning; no rider is there;
But its bridle is red with the sign of despair.
Weep! Albin, to death and captivity led,
Oh weep, but thy tears cannot number the dead;
For a merciless sword on Culloden shall wave,
Culloden! that reeks with the blood of the brave.

#### LOCHIEL.

Go preach to the coward, thou death telling seer!
Or, if gory Culloden so dreadful appear,
Draw, dotard, around thy old wavering sight,
This mantle, to cover the phantom of fright.

#### WIZARD.

Ha, laughest thou, Lochiel, my vision to scorn,
Proud bird of the mountain, thy plume shall be torn.

Say, rushed the bold eagle exultingly forth,
From his home in the dark rolling clouds of the north?
Lo! the death shot of foemen out-speeding, he rode
Companionless, bearing destruction abroad.
But down let him stoop from his havoc on high !
Ah! home let him speed, for the spoiler is nigh.
Why flames the far summit! Why shoot to the blast
Those embers, like stars from the firmament cast?
'Tis the fire shower of ruin, all dreadfully driven
From his aeric that beacons the darkness of heaven.
Oh crested Lochiel! the peerless in might,
Whose banners arise on the battlements' hight;
Heaven's fire is around thee, to blast and to burn;
Return to thy dwelling! all lonely return !
For the blackness of ashes shall mark where it stood,
And a wild mother scream o'er her famishing brood.

#### LOCHIEL.

False Wizard, avaunt! I have marshaled my clan ;
Their swords are a thousand, their bosoms are one !
They are true to the last of their blood and their breath,
And like reapers descend to the harvest of death.
Then welcome be Cumberland's steed to the shock!
Let him dash his proud foam like a wave on the rock!
But woe to his kindred, and woe to his cause,
When Albin her claymore indignantly draws.
When her bonneted Chieftains to victory crowd,
Clan Ranald the dauntless, and Moray the proud,
All plaided and plumed in their tartan array—

#### WIZARD.

———Lochiel, Lochiel, beware of the day !
For, dark and despairing my sight I may seal,
But man cannot cover what God would reveal;
'Tis the sunset of life gives me mystical lore,
And coming events cast their shadows before.
I tell thee Culloden's dread echoes shall ring,
With the bloodhounds that bark for thy fugitive king.
Lo, annointed by heaven with vials of wrath,
Behold, where he flies on his desolate path !
Now, in darkness and billows, he sweeps from my sight;
Rise! rise! ye wild tempests, and cover his flight!

'Tis finished! their thunders are hushed on the moors,
Culloden is lost and my country deplores:
But where is the iron bound prisoner? Where?
For the red eye of battle is shut in despair.
Say, mounts he the ocean wave, banished, forlorn,
Like a limb from his country, cast bleeding and torn?
Ah no! for a darker departure is near;
The war drum is muffled, and black is the bier;
His death bell is tolling; oh! mercy! dispel
Yon sight that it feezes my spirit to tell!
Life flutters convulsed in his quivering limbs,
And his blood-streaming nostril in agony swims.
Accursed be the faggots that blaze at his feet,
Where his heart shall be thrown, ere it ceases to beat,
With the smoke of its ashes to poison the gale—

### LOCHIEL.

——————Down, soothless insulter! I trust not the tale,
Though my perishing ranks should be strewed in their gore
Like ocean weeds heaped on the surf-beaten shore,
Lochiel, untainted by flight or by chains,
While the kindling of life in his bosom remains,
Shall victor exult, or in death be laid low,
With his back to the field, and his feet to the foe!
And leaving in battle no blot on his name,
Look proudly to heaven from the death bed of fame.

# TAM O'SHANTER.

### ROBERT BURNS.

When chapman billies leave the street,
And drouthy neibors neibors meet,
As market days are wearin' late,
And folk begin to tak the gate;
While we sit bousing at the nappy,
And gettin' fou and unco happy,
We think na on the lang Scots miles,
The mosses, waters, slaps, and stiles,
That lie between us and our hame,

Whare sits our sulky sullen dame,
Gathering her brows like gathering storm,
Nursing her wrath to keep it warm.

This truth fand honest Tam o'Shanter,
As he frae Ayr ae night did canter,
(Auld Ayr, wham ne'er a town surpasses
For honest men and bonny lasses.)

O Tam ! hadst thou but been sae wise
As ta'en thy ain wife Kate's advice !
She tauld thee weel thou wast a skellum,
A blethering, blustering, drunken blellum,
That frae November till October,
Ae market day thou wasna sober;
That ilka melder, wi' the miller
Thou sat as lang as thou hadst siller;
That every naig was ca'd a shoe on,
The smith and thee gat roaring fou on;
That at the Lord's house, even on Sunday,
Thou drank wi' Kirkton Jean till Monday,
She prophesied that, late or soon,
Thou wouldst be found deep drown'd in Doon!
Or catch'd wi' warlocks i' the mirk,
By Alloway's auld haunted kirk.

Ah, gentle dames! it gars me greet
To think how mony counsels sweet,
How mony lengthen'd sage advices,
The hurband frae the wife despises!

But to our tale:—Ae market night,
Tam had got planted unco right,
Fast by an ingle, bleezing finely,
Wi' reaming swats, that drank divinely;
And at his elbow Souter Johnny,
His ancient, trusty, drouthy crony;
Tam lo'ed him like a vera brither—
They had been fou for weeks thegither!
The night they drave on wi' sangs and clatter,
And aye the ale was growing better;
The landlady and Tam grew gracious,
Wi' favours secret, sweet, and precious;

The Souter tauld his queerest stories,
The landlord's laugh was ready chorus:
The storm without might rair and rustle—
Tam didna mind the storm a whistle.

Care, mad to see a man sae happy,
E'en drown'd himsel amang the nappy!
As bees flee hame wi' lades of treasure,
The minutes wing'd their way wi' pleasure:
Kings may be blessed, but Tam was glorious,
O'er a' the ills o' life victorious!
But pleasures are like poppies spread,
You seize the flower, its bloom is shed!
Or like the snowfall in the river,
A moment white—then melts forever;
Or like the borealis race,
That flit ere you can point their place;
Or like the rainbow's lovely form,
Evanishing amid the storm.
Nae man can tether time or tide;
The hour approaches Tam maun ride;
That hour o' night's black arch the keystane,
That dreary hour he mounts his beast in;
And sic a night he taks the road in
As ne'r poor sinner was abroad in.

The wind blew as 'twad blawn its last;
The rattling showers rose on the blast;
The speedy gleams the darkness swallow'd;
Loud, deep, and lang the thunder bellow'd:
That night, a child might understand
The deil had business on hie hand.

Weel mounted on his gray mare, Meg,
A better never lifted leg,
Tam skelpit on through dub and mire,
Despising wind, and rain, and fire;
Whiles holding fast his guid blue bonnet,
Whiles crooning o'er some auld Scots sonnet;
Whiles glowering round wi' prudent cares,
Lest bogles catch him unawares,
Kirk Alloway was drawing nigh,
Where ghaists and houlets nightly cry.

By this time he was 'cross the foord,
Whare in the snaw the chapman smoor'd;
And past the birks and meikle stane,
Whare drunken Charlie brak's neckbane:
And througn the whins, and by the cairn
Whare hunters fand the murder'd bairn;
And near the thorn, aboon the well,
Whare Mungo's mither hang'd hersel.
Before him Doon pours a' his floods;
The doubling storm roars through the woods;
The lightnings flash frae pole to pole;
Near and more near the thunders roll;
When, glimmering through the groaning trees,
Kirk-Alloway seem'd in a bleeze;
Through ilka bore the beams were glancing,
And loud resounded mirth and dancing.

Inspiring bold John Barleycorn!
What dangers thou canst mak us scorn!
Wi' tippeny, we fear nae evil;
Wi' usquebae, we'll face the devil!—
The swat sae ream'd in Tammie's noddle,
Fair play, he cared na deils a boddle.
But Maggie stood right sair astonish'd,
Till, by the heel and hand admonish'd,
She ventured forward on the light,
And, wow! Tam saw an unco sight!
Warlocks and witches in a dance;
Nae cotillon brent-new frae France;
But hornpipes, jigs, strathspeys, and reels,
Put life and mettle i' their heels:
At winnock-bunker, i' the east,
There sat auld Nick, in shape o' beast;
A towzie tyke, black, grim, and large,
To gie them music was his charge:
He screw'd the pipes, and girt them skirl,
Till roof and rafters a' did dirl.
Coffins stood round, like open presses,
That shaw'd the dead in their last dresses,
And by some devilish cantrip slight
Each in his cauld hand held a light,—

By which heroic Tam was able,
To note upon the haly table,
A murderer's banes in gibbet airns;
Twa span lang, wee, unchristen'd bairns;
A thief, new-cutted frae a rape,
Wi' his last gasp his gab did gape;
Five tomahawks wi' bluid red-rusted;
Five scimitars, wi' murder crusted;
A garter, which a babe had strangled;
A knife, a father's throat had mangled,
Whom his ain son o' life bereft,
The gray hairs yet stack to the heft:

    \*     \*     \*     \*     \*

Wi' mair o' horrible and awfu',
Which even to name wad be unlawfu'.

As Tammie glower'd, amazed and curious,
The mirth and fun grew fast and furious:
The piper loud and louder blew,
The dancers quick and quicker flew;
They reel'd, they set, they crossed, they cleekit,
Till ilka carlin swat and reekit,
And coost her duddies to the wark,
And linket at it in her sark.

Now Tam! O Tam! had thae been queans,
A' plump and strappin' in their teens,
Their sarks, instead o' creeshie flannen,
Been snaw-white seventeen-hunder linen!
Thir breeks o' mine, my only pair,
That ance were plush, o' gued blue hair,
I wad hae gien them aff my hurdies,
For ae blink o' the bonny burdies!

But wither'd beldams, auld and droll,
Rigwoodie hags, wad spean a foal,
Lowpin' and flingin' on a cummock,
I wonder didna turn thy stomach.

But Tam kenn'd what was what fu' brawlie,
"There was ae winsome wench and walie,"
That night enlisted in the core,

(Lang after kenn'd on Carrick shore,
For mony a beast to dead she shot,
And perish'd mony a bonny boat,
And shook baith meikle corn and bear,
And kept the country side in fear.)
Her cutty sark, o' Paisley harn,
That, while a lassie she hed worn,
In longitude though sorely scanty,
It was her best, and she was vauntie.

Ah! little kenn'd thy reverend grannie,
That sark she coft for her wee Nannie,
Wi' twa pund Scots, ('twas a' her riches,)
Wad ever graced a dance o' witches!

But here my Muse her wing maun cour,
Sic flights are far beyond her power;
To sing how Nannie lap and flang,
(A souple jade she was and strang,)
And how Tam stood, like ane bewitch'd,
And thought his very cen enrich'd;
Even Satan glower'd, and fidged fu' fain,
And hotched'd and blew wi' might and main:
Till first ae caper, syne anither,
Tam tint his reason a' thegither,
And roars out "Weel done, Cutty sark!"
And in an instant a' was dark:
And scarcely had he Maggie rallied,
When out the hellish legion sallied.
As bees bizz out wi' angry fyke,
When plundering herds assail their byke,
As open pussie's mortal foes,
When pop! she starts before their nose;
As eager runs the market-crowd,
When "Catch the thief!" resounds aloud;
So Maggie runs, the witches follow,
Wi' mony an eldritch screech and hollow.

Ah Tam! ah Tam! thou'lt get thy fairin'!
In hell they'll roast thee like a herrin'!
In vain thy Kate awaits thy comin'!
Kate soon will be a wofu' woman!

Now, do thy speedy utmost, Meg,
And win the keystane of the brig;
There at them thou thy tail may toss,
A running stream they darena cross;
But ere the keystane she could make
The fient a tail had she to shake!
For Nannie, far before the rest,
Hard upon noble Maggie prest,
And flew at Tam wi' furious ettle:
But little wist she Maggie's mettle—
Ae spring brought off her master hale,
But left behind her ain gray tail;
The carlin caught her by the rump,
And left poor Maggie scarce a stump.

Now, wha this tale o' truth shall read,
Ilk man and mother's son, take heed:
Whane'er to drink you are inclined,
Or Cutty-sarks run in your mind,
Think! ye may buy the joys owre dear—
Remember Tam o' Shanter's mare.

## TWA DOGS.

### ROBERT BURNS.

'Twas in that place o' Scotland's isle,
That bears the name o' auld King Coil,
Upon a bonny day in June,
When wearing through the afternoon,
Twa dogs that werena thrang at hame,
Forgather'd ance upon a time.

The first I'll name, they ca'd him Cæsar,
Was keepit for his honour's pleasure:
His hair, his size, his mouth, his lugs,
Show'd he was nane o' Scotland's dogs;
But whalpit some place far abroad,
Where sailors gang to fish for cod.

His locked, letter'd, braw brass collar
Show'd him the gentleman and scholar;
But thou he was o' high degree,
The fient a pride—nae pride had he;
But wad hae spent an hour caressin',
Even wi' a tinkler-gypsy's messan:
At kirk or market, mill or smiddie,
Nae tawted tyke, though e'er sae duddie,
But he wad stan't, as glad to see him,
And stroan't on stanes and hillocks wi' him.

The tither was a ploughman's collie,
A rhyming, ranting, roving billie,
Wha for his friend and comrade had him,
And in his freaks had Luath ca'd him,
After some dog in Highland sang,
Was made lang syne—Lord knaws how lang.

He was a gash and faithfu' tyke,
As ever lap a sheugh or dike.
His honest sonsie, baws'nt face,
Aye gat him friends in ilka place.
His breast was white, his tousie back
Weel clad wi' coat o' glossy black;
His gaucie tail, wi' upward curl,
Hung o'er his hurdies wi' a swirl.

Nae doubt but they were fain o' ither,
And unco pack and thick thegither;
Wi' social nose whyles snuff'd and snowkit,
Whyles mice and moudieworts they howkit;
Whyles scour'd awa' in lang excursion,
And worried ither in diversion;
Until wi' daffin' weary grown,
Upon a knowe they sat them down,
And there began a lang digression
About the lords o' the creation.

CÆSAR.

I've often wonder'd, honest Luath,
What sort o' life poor dogs like you have,
And when the gentry's life I saw,
What way poor bodies lived ava.

Our laird gets in his racked rents,
His coals, his kain, and a' his stents;
He rises when he likes himsel;
His flunkies answer at the bell;
He ca's his coach, he ca's his horse;
He draws a bonny silken purse
As 'ang's my tail, whare, through the steeks,
The yellow-letter'd Geordie keeks.

Frae morn to e'en it's nought but toiling,
At baking, roasting, frying, boiling;
And though the gentry first are stetchin,
Yet e'en the ha' folk fill their pechan
Wi' sauce, ragouts, and siclike trashtrie,
That's little short o' downright wastrie,
Our whipper-in, we, blastit wonner,
Poor worthless elf, it eats a dinner
Better than ony tenant man
His honour has in a' the lan';
And what poor cot-folk pit their painch in,
I own it's past my comprehension.

LUATH.

Trowth, Cæsar, whyles they're fasht eneugh;
A cotter howkin' in a sheugh,
Wi' dirty stanes biggin' a dike,
Baring a quarry, and siclike;
Himsel, his wife, he thus sustains,
A smytrie o' wee duddie weans,
And naught but his han' darg to keep
Them right and tight in thack and rape.

And when they meet wi' sair disasters,
Like loss o' health or want o' masters,
Ye maist wad think, a wee touch langer,
And they maun starve o' cauld and hunger;
But how it comes I never kenn'd yet,
They're maistly wonderfu' contented;
And buirdly chiels, and clever hizzies,
Are bred in sic a way as this is.

CÆSAR.

But then to how ye're negleckit,

How huff'd, and cuff'd, and disrespeckit!
Lord, man, our gentry care as little
For delvers, ditchers, and sic cattle;
They gang as saucy by poor folk
As I wad by a stinkin' brock.
I've noticed, on our laird's court-day,
And mony a time my heart's been wae,
Poor tenant bodies, scant o' cash,
How they maun thole a factor's snash :
He'll stamp and threaten, curse and swear;
He'll apprehend them, poind their gear;
While they maun stan', wi' aspect humble,
And hear it a', and fear and tremble!

I see how folk live that hae riches;
But surely poor folk maun be wretches!

### LUATH.

They're no sae wretched 's ane wad think;
Though constantly on poortith's brink :
They're sae accustom'd wi' the sight,
The view o't gies them little fright.

Then chance and fortune are sae guided,
They're aye in less or mair provided;
And though fatigued wi' close employment,
A blink o' rest's a sweet enjoyment.

The dearest comfort o' their lives,
Their gushie weans and faithfu' wives;
The prattling things are just their pride,
That sweetens a' their fire-side;
And whyles twalpennie worth o' nappy
Can mak the bodies unco happy;
They lay aside their private cares,
To mind the Kirk and state affairs:
They'll talk o' patronage and priests
Wi kindling fury in their breasts;
Or tell what new taxation's comin',
And ferlie at the folk in Lun'on.

As bleak-faced Hallowmas returns,
They get the jovial ranting kirns,

When rural life o' every station
Unite in common recreation;
Love blinks, Wit slaps, and social Mirth
Forgets there's Care upo' the earth.

That merry day the year begins
They bar the door on frosty win's;
The nappy recks wi' mantling ream,
And sheds a heart-inspiring steam;
The luntin pipe and sneeshin mill
Are handed round wi' right guid will;
The cantie auld folks crackin' crouse,
The young anes rantin' through the house,—
My heart has been sae fain to see them,
That I for joy hae barkit wi' them.

Still it's owre true that ye hae said,
Sic game is now owre aften play'd,
There's mony a creditable stock
O' decent, honest, fawsont folk,
Are riven out baith root and branch,
Some rascal's pridefu' greed to quench,
Wha thinks knit himsel the faster
In favour wi' some gentle master,
Wha aiblins thrang a parliamentin'
For Britain's guide his saul indentin'—

### CÆSAR.

Faith, lad, ye little ken about it;
For Britain's guid! guid faith, I doubt it.
Say rather, gaun as Premiers lead him;
And saying Ay or No's they bid him:
At operas and plays parading,
Mortgaging, gambling, masquerading,
Or maybe, in a frolic daft,
To Hague or Calais taks a waft,
To make a tour, and tak a whirl,
To learn *bon ton*, and see the worl'.

There, at Vienna or Versailles,
He rives his father's auld entails;
Or by Madrid he takes the route,

To thrum guitars, and fecht wi' nowte;
Or down the Italian vista startles,
Whore-hunting among groves o' myrtles,
Then bouses drumly German water,
To mak himsel look fair and fatter,
And clear the consequential sorrows,
Love gifts of Carnival signoras.
For Britain's guid!—for her destruction!
Wi' dissipation, feud and faction!

### LUATH.

Hech man! dear sirs! is that the gate
They waste sae mony a braw estate!
Are we sae foughten and harrass'd
For gear to gang that gate at last!

Oh, would they stay aback fra courts,
And please themselves wi' country sports,
It wad for every ane be better,
The Laird, The Tenant, and the Cotter!
For thae frank, rantin' ramblin' billies,
Fient haet o' them's ill-hearted fellows;
Except for breakin' o' their timmer,
Or speakin lightly o' their limmer,
Or shootin' o' a hare or moorcock,
The ne'er a bit they'er ill to poor folk.

But will ye tell me Master Caesar,
Sure great folk's life's a life o' pleasure?
Nae cauld nor hunger e'er can steer them,
The very thought o't needna fear them.

### CAESAR.

Lord, man, were ye but whyles whare I am,
The gentles ye wad ne'er envy 'em.
It's true they needna starve nor sweat,
Through winter's cauld or simmer's heat;
They've nae sair wark to craze their banes,
And fill auld age wi' grips and granes:
But human bodies are sic fools,
For a' their colleges and schools
That when nae real ills perplex them,

They mak enow themsels to vex them;
And aye the less they hae to sturt them,
In like proportion less will hurt them.

A country fellow at the pleugh,
His acres till'd he's right eneugh;
A country girl at her wheel,
Her dizzens done, she's unco weel:
But Gentlemen, and Ladies warst,
Wi' evendown want o' wark are curst.
They loiter, lounging, lank, and lazy;
Though deil haet ails them, yet uneasy;
Their days insipid, dull and tasteless;
Their nights unquiet, lang, and restless;
And e'en their sports, their balls and races,
Their galloping through public places,
There's sic parade, sic pomp and art,
The joy can scarcely reach the heart.

The men cast out in party matches,
Then sowther a' in deep debauches;
Ae night they'er mad wi' drink and whoring,
Neist day their life is past enduring.

The Ladies arm-in-arm in clusters,
As great and gracious a' as sisters,
But hear their absent thoughts o' ither,
They'ae a' run deils and jades thegither.
Whyles, owre the wee bit cup and platie,
They sip the scandal potion pretty:
Or lee-lang nights, wi' crabbit lukes,
Pore ower the devil's pictured beuks;
Stake on a chance a farmer's stackyard,
And cheat like ony unhanged blackguard.
There's some exception, man and woman;
But this is Gentry's life in common.

By this, the sun was out o' sight,
And darker gloaming brought the night:
The bum-clock hummed wi' lazy drone;
The kye stood rowtin i' the loan:
When up they gat and shook their lugs,

Rejoiced they werena men, but dogs;
And each took aff his several way,
Resolved to meet some ither day.

## THE COTTER'S SATURDAY NIGHT.

ROBERT BURNS.

My loved, my honor'd, much respected friend!
  No mercenary bard his homage pays;
With honest pride, I scorn each selfish end:
  My dearest meed, a friend's esteem and praise,
To you I sing, in simple Scottish lays,
  The lowly train in life's sequester'd scene;
The native feelings strong, the guileless ways:
  What Aiken in a cottage would have been;
Ah! though his worth unknown, far happier there,
    I ween!

November chill blaws loud wi' angry sugh;
  The short'ning winter-day is near a close;
The miry beasts retreating frae the plough;
  The black'ning trains o' craws to their repose;
The toil-worn cotter frae his labor goes,
  This night his weekly moil is at an end,
Collects his spades, his mattocks, and his hoes,
  Hoping the morn in ease and rest to spend,
And weary, o'er the moor his course does hameward
    bend.

At length his lonely cot appears in view
  Beneath the shelter of an aged tree;
Th' expectant wee things, toddlin', stacher through
  To meet their dad, wi' flichterin noise and glee.
His wee bit ingle, blinking bonnily,
  His clean hearthstone, his thrifty wifie's smile,
The lisping infant prattling on his knee,
  Does a' his weary carking cares beguile,
And makes him quite forget his labor and his toil.

Belyve, the elder bairns come drapping in,

At service out among the farmers roun':
Some ca' the pleugh, some herd, some tentie rin
   A caunie errand to a neibor town:
Their eldest hope, their Jenny, woman grown,
   In youthfu' bloom, love sparkling in her ee,
Comes hame, perhaps to show a braw new gown,
   Or deposit her sair-won penny fee,
To help her parents dear, if they in hardship be.

Wi' joy unfeign'd, brothers and sisters meet,
   And each for other's welfare kindly spiers:
The social hours, swift-wing'd unnoticed, fleet;
   Each tells the uncos that he sees or hears;
The parents, partial, eye their hopeful years;
   Anticipation forward points the view.
The mother, wi' her needle and her shears,
   Gars auld claes look amaist as weel's the new—
The father mixes a' wi' admonition due.

Their master's and their mistress's command,
   The younkers a' are warned to obey;
And mind their labours wi' an eydent hand,
   And ne'er, though out of sight jauk or play:
"And oh! be sure to fear the Lord alway!
   And mind your duty, duly morn and night!
Lest in temptation's path ye gang astray,
   Implore His counsel and assisting might:
They never sought in vain who sought the Lord
      aright!"

But, hark! a rap comes gently to the door,
   Jenny, wha kens the meaning o' the same,
Tells how a neibor lad cam o'er the moor,
   To do some errands, and convoy her hame.
The wily mother sees the conscious flame
   Sparkle in Jenny's ee, and flush her cheek,
Wi' heart struck anxious care, inquires his name,
   While Jenny hafflins is afraid to speak;
Weel pleased the mother hears it's nae wild, worth-
      less rake.

Wi' kindly welcome, Jenny brings him ben;

A strappin' youth; he takes the mother's eye;
Blithe Jenny sees the visit's no ill ta'en;
The father cracks of horses, ploughs, and kye,
The youngster's artless heart o'erflows wi' joy,
But blate and lathefu', scarce can weel behave;
The mother, wi' a woman's wiles, can spy
What makes the youth sae bashfu' and sae grave;
Weel pleased to think her bairn's respected like the
    lave.

Oh happy love!—where love like this is found!—
Oh heart-felt raptures!—bliss beyond compare!
I've paced much this weary, mortal round,
And sage experience bids me this declare—
"If Heaven a draught of heavenly pleasure spare,
One cordial in this melancholy vale,
'Tis when a youthful, loving, modest pair,
In others arms, breathe out the tender tale,
Beneath the milk-white thorn, that scents the even-
    ing gale."

Is there in human form, that bears a heart,
A wretch! a villain! lost to love and truth!
That can, with studied, sly ensnaring art,
Betray sweet Jennie's unsuspecting youth?
Curse on his perjured arts! dissembling smooth!
Are honor, virtue, conscience, all exiled?
Is there no pity, no relenting ruth,
Points to the parents fondling o'er their child?
Then paints the ruined maid, and their distraction
    wild!

But now the supper crowns their simple board,
The halesome parritch, chief of Scotia's food:
The soupe their only hawkie does afford,
That 'yont the hallan snugly chows her cood:
The dame brings forth, in complimental mood,
To grace the lad, her weel-hain'd kebbuck, fell,
And aft he's prest, and aft he ca's it guid:
The frugal wifie, garrulous, will tell,
How 'twas townmon auld, sin' lint was 'i the bell.

The cheerfu' supper done, wi' serious face,
 They, round the ingle, form a circle wide;
The sire turns o'er, wi' patriarchal grace,
 The big ha' Bible, ance his father's pride;
His bonnet rev'rently is laid aside,
 His lyart haffets wearing thin and bare;
Those strains that once did sweet in Zion glide,
 He wales a portion with judicious care;
And "Let us worship God," he says, with solemn air.

They chant their artless notes in simple guise;
 They tune their hearts, by far the noblest aim:
Perhaps "Dundee's" wild-warbling measures rise,
 Or plaintive "Martyrs," worthy of the name;
Or noble "Elgin" beets the heaven-ward flame,
 The sweetest far of Scotia's holy lays:
Compared with these, Italian trills are tame;
 The tickled ear no heartfelt raptures raise;
Nae unison hae they with our creator's praise.

The priest-like father reads the sacred page,
 How Abram was the friend of God on high;
Or, Moses bade eternal warfare wage
 With Amalek's ungracious progeny;
Or how the royal bard did groaning lie
 Beneath the stroke of Heaven's avenging ire,
Or Job's pathetic plaint, and wailing cry;
 Or rapt Isaiah's wild seraphic fire;
Or other holy seers that tune the sacred lyre.

Perhaps the Christain volume is the theme,
 How guiltless blood for guilty man was shed;
How He, who bore in heaven the second name,
 Had not on earth whereon to lay His head:
How His first followers and servants sped;
 The precepts sage they wrote to many a land:
How he, who lone in Patmos banish'd,
 Saw in the sun a mighty angel stand;
And heard great Bab'lon's doom pronounced by
 Heaven's command.

Then kneeling down, to HEAVEN'S ETERNAL KING,

The saint, the father, and the husband prays:
Hope "springs exulting on triumpoant wing,"
    That thus they all shall meet in future days:
There ever bask in uncreated rays,
    No more to sigh or shed the bitter tear,
Together hymning their Creator's praise,
    In such society, yet still more dear;
While circling time moves round in an eternal sphere.

Compared with this, how poor religion's pride,
    In all the pomp of method and of art,
When men display to congregations wide
    Devotion's every grace, except the heart!
The Power, incensed, the pageant will desert
    The pompous strain, the sacerdotal stole:
But, haply, in some cottage far apart,
    May hear, well pleased, the language of the soul;
And in his book of life the inmates poor enrol.

Then homeward all take off their several way;
    The youngling cottagers retire to rest;
The parent-pair their secret homage pay,
    And proffer up to heaven the warm request
That HE, who stills the raven's clamorous nest,
    And decks the lily fair in flowery pride,
Would, in the way His wisdom sees the best,
    For them and for their little ones provide;
But chiefly, in their hearts with grace divine preside.

From scenes like these old Scotia's grandeur springs,
    That makes her loved at home, revered abroad:
Princes and lords are but the breath of kings,
    "An honest man's the noblest work of GOD,"
And certes, in fair virtue's heavenly road,
    The cottage leaves the palace far behind.
What is a lordling's pomp?—a cumbrous load,
    Disguising oft the wretch of human kind,
Studied in arts of hell, in wickedness refined!

O Scotia! my dear, my native soil!
    For whom my warmest wish to Heaven is sent!
Long may thy hardy sons of rustic toil,

Be blest with health, and peace; and sweet content!

And, oh! may Heaven their simple lives prevent
    From luxury's contagion, weak and vile!
Then, howe'er crown and coronets be rent,
    A virtuous populace may rise the while,
And stand a wall of fire around their much-loved isle.

O thou! who pour'd the patriotic tide
    That stream'd through Wallace's undaunted heart;
Who dared to nobly stem tyrannic pride,
    Or nobly die, the second glorious part,
(The patriot's God, peculiarly Thou art,
    His friend, inspirer, guardian, and reward!)
Oh, never, never, Scotia's realm desert;
    But still the patriot and the patriot-bard,
In bright succession rise, her ornament and guard!

## THE BRIGS OF AYR.

### ROBERT BURNS.

The simple bard, rough at the rustic plough,
Learning his tuneful trade from every bough;
The chatting linnet, or the mellow thrush,
Hailing the setting sun, sweet, in the green-thorn bush;
The soaring lark, the perching redbreast shrill,
Or deep-toned plovers, gray, wild-whistling o'er the hill;
Shall he, nurst in the peasant's lowly shed,
To hardy independence bravely bred,
By early poverty to hardship steel'd,
And train'd to arms in stern Misfortune's field—
Shall he be guilty of their hireling crimes,
The servile, mercenary Swiss of rhymes?
Or labour hard the panegyric close,
With all the venal soul of dedicating prose?
No! though his artless strains he rudely sings,
And throws his hand uncouthly o'er the strings,
He glows with all the spirit of the bard,
Fame, honest fame, his great, his dear reward!
Still, if some patron's generous care he trace,

Skill'd in the secret, to bestow with grace;
When Ballantyne befriends his humble name,
And hands the rustic stranger up to fame,
With heart-felt throes his grateful bosom swells,
The god-like bliss, to give, alone excells.

'Twas when the stacks got on their winter hap,
And thack and rape secure the toilwon crap;
Potato-bings are snugged up frae skaith
O' coming Winter's biting, frosty breath;
The bees, rejoicing o'er their summer toils,
Unnumber'd buds and flowers' delicious spoils
Seal'd up with frugal care in massive waxen piles,
Are doom'd by man, that tyrant o'er the weak,
The death o' devils, smoor'd wi' brimstone reek:
The thundering guns are heard on every side,
The wounded coveys, reeling, scatter wide,
The feather'd field-mates, bound by Nature's tie,
Sires, mothers, children, in one carnage lie,
(What warm, poetic heart, but inly bleeds,
And execrates man's savage, ruthless deeds!)
Nae mair the flower in field or meadow springs,
Nae mair the grove with airy concert rings,
Except, perhaps, the robin's whistling glee,
Proud o' the height o' some bit half lang tree:
The hoary morns precede the sunny days,
Mild, calm, serene, wide spreads the noontide blaze,
While thick the gossamer waves wanton in the rays.

'Twas in that season, when a simple bard,
Unknown and poor, simplicity's reward,
Ae night, within the ancient brugh of Ayr,
By whim inspired, or haply prest wi' care,
He left his bed and took his wayward route,
And down by Simpson's wheel'd the left about:
(Whether impell'd by all directing Fate,
To witness what I after shall narrate;
Or penitential pangs for former sins,
Led him to rove by quondam Merran Dins;
Or whether, rapt in meditation high,
He wander'd out, he knew not where nor why)

The drowsy Dungeon clock had number'd two,
And Wallace Tower had sworn the fact was true:
The tide-swoln Firth, wi' sullen sounding roar,
Through the still night dash'd hoarse along the shore.
All else was hush'd as Nature's closed ee:
The silent moon shone high o'er tower and tree:
The chilly frost, beneath their silver beam,
Crept, gently-crusting, o'er the glittering stream.

When, lo! on either hand the listening bard,
The clanging sugh of whistling wings is heard;
Two dusky forms dart through the midnight air
Swift as the gos drives on the wheeling hare;
Ane on the Auld Brig his airy shape uprears,
The ither flutters o'er the rising piers;
Our warlock rhymer instantly descried
The sprites that owre the Brigs of Ayr preside,
(That bards are second-sighted is nae joke,
And ken the lingo of the spiritual folk;
Fays, spunkies, kelpies, a', they can explain them,
And even the very deils they brawly ken them.
Auld Brig appear'd o' ancient Pictish race,
The very wrinkles Gothic in his face;
He seem'd as he wi' Time had warstled lang,
Yet, teughly doure, he bade an unco bang
New Brig was buskit in a braw new coat,
That he at Lun'on frae ane Adams got;
In's hand five taper staves as smooth's a bead,
Wi' virls and wirlygigums at the head.
The Goth was stalking round with anxious search,
Spying the time-worn flaws in every arch;—
It chanced his new-come neibor took his ee,
And e'en a vex'd and angry heart had he!
Wi' thieveless sneer to see his modish mien,
He, down the water, gies him this guid e'en:— •

### AULD BRIG.

    I doubt na frien', ye'll think ye're nae sheep-shank,
Ance ye wore streekit owre frae bank to bank!
But gin ye be a brig as auld as me—
Though, faith, that date I doubt ye'll never see—
There'll be, if that date come, I'll wad a boddle,

Some fewer whigmaleeries in your noddle.

NEW BRIG.

Auld Vandal, ye but show your little mense,
Just much about it, wi' your scanty sense;
Will your poor narrow footpath of a street—
When twa wheelbarrows tremble when they meet—
Your ruin'd, formless bulk o' stane and lime,
Compare wi' bonny brigs o' modern time,
There's men o' taste would tak the Ducat stream,
Though they should cast the very sark and swim
Ere they would grate their feelings wi' the view
O' sic an ugly gothic hulk as you.

AULD BRIG.

Conceited gowk! puff'd up wi windy pride!
This mony a year I've stood the flood and tide;
And though wi' crazy eild I'm sair forfairn,
I'll be a brig when ye're a shapeless cairn!
As yet ye little ken about the matter,
But twa-three winters will inform ye better.
When heavy, dark, continued, a'-day rains,
Wi' deepening deluge, o'erflow the plains,
When from the hills where springs the brawling Coil,
Or stately Lugar's mossy fountains boil,
Or where the Greenock winds his moorland course,
Or haunted Garpel draws his feeble source,
Aroused by blustering winds and spotting thowes,
In mony a torrent down his snaw-broo rowes;
While crashing ice, borne on the roaring spate,
Sweeps dams, and mills, and brigs a' to the gate:
And from Glenbuck, down to the Ratton-key,
Auld Ayr is just one lengthen'd tumbling sea—
Then down ye'll hurl, deil nor ye never rise!
And dash the gumlie jaups up to the pouring skies.
A lesson sadly teaching, to your cost,
That Architecture's noble art is lost!

NEW BRIG.

Fine Architecture, troth, I needs must say o't,
The Lord be thankit that we've tint the gate o't!
Gaunt, ghastly, ghaist-alluring edifices,
Hanging with threatening jut, like precipices,

O'crarching, mouldy, gloom-inspiring coves,
Supporting roofs fantastic, stony groves;
Windows and doors, in nameless sculpture drest,
With order, symmetry, or taste unblest;
Forms like some bedlam statuary's dream,
The crazed creations of misguided whim;
Forms might be worship'd on the bended knee,
And still the second dead command be free,
Their likeness is not found on earth, in air, or sea.
Mansions that would disgrace the building taste
Of any mason reptile, bird, or beast;
Fit only for a doited monkish race,
Or frosty maids foresworn the dear embrace:
Or cuifs of later times wha held the notion
That sullen gloom was sterling true devotion;
Fancies that our guid brugh denies protection !
And soon may they expire, unblest with resurrection !

ACLD BRIG.

O ye, my dear-remember'd ancient yealings,
Were ye but here to share my wounded feelings!
Ye worthy proveses, and mony a bailie,
Wha in tha paths o' righteousness did toil aye;
Ye dainty deacons, and ye douce conveeners
To whom our moderns are but causeycleaners !
Ye godly councils wha hae blest this town;
Ye godly brethren o' the sacred gown,
Wha meekly gae your hurdies to the smiters;
And (what would now be strange) ye godly writers;
A' ye douce folk I've born aboon the broo,
Were ye but here, what would ye say or do!
How would your spirits groan in deep vexation
To see each melancholy alteration;
And, agonizing, curse the time and place
When ye begat the base, degenerate race !
Nae langer reverend men, their country's glory,
In plain braid Scots hold forth a plain braid story !
Nae langer thrifty citizens and douce,
Meet owre a pint, or in the council-house;
But staumrel, corkey-headed, graceless gentry,
The berryment and ruin of the country;

Men three parts made by tailors and by barbers,    [bors!
Wha waste your weel-hain'd on damn'd new brigs and har-

NEW BRIG.

Now haud you there! for faith ye've said enough,
And muckle mair then ye can mak to through;
That's aye a string auld doited gray-beards harp on,
A topic for their peevishness to carp on.
As for your priesthood, I shall say but little,
Corbies and clergy are a shot right kittle;
But, under favour o' your langer beard,
Abuse o' magistrates might weel be spared,
To liken them to your auld-warld squad,    .
I must needs say comparisons are odd.
In Ayr, wag-wits nae mair can hae a handle
To mouth "a citzen" a term o' scandal;
Nae mair the council waddles down the street,
In all the pomp of ignorant conceit;
No difference but bulkiest or tallest,
With comforable dullness in for ballast;
Nor shoals nor currents need a pilot's caution,
For regularly slow, they only witness motion;
Men wha grew wise priggin' owre hops and raisins,
Or gather'd liberal views in bonds and seisins,
If haply Knowledge, on a random tramp,
Had shorde them wi' a glimmer of his lamp,
And would to Common Sense for once betray'd them,
Plain, dull Stupidity stept kindly in to aid them.
    What further clishmaclaver might been said,
What bloody wars, if sprites had blood to shed;
No man can tell; but all before their sight,
A fairy train appear'd in order bright;
Adown the glittering stream they featly danced;
Bright to the moon their various dresses glanced:
They footed o'er the watery glass so neat,
The infant ice scarce bent beneath their feet;
While arts of minstrelsy among them rung,
And soul-ennobling bards heroic ditties sung.
Oh, had M'Lachlan, thairm-inspiring sage,
Been there to hear this heavenly band engage, [land rage:
When through his dear stratslpeys they bore with High-

Or when they struck old Scotia's melting airs,
The lover's raptured joys or bleeding cares;
How would his Highland lug been nobler fired,
And even his matchless hand with finer touch inspired!
No guess could tell what instrument appear'd,
But all the soul of Music's self was heard;
Harmonious concert rung in every part,
While simple melody pour'd moving on the heart.

The Genius of the stream in front appears,
A venerable chief advanced in years;
His hoary head with water-lilies crown'd,
His manly leg with garter-tangle bound.
Next came the loveliest pair in all the ring,
Sweet Female Beauty hand in hand with Spring;
Then, crown'd with flowery hay, came Rural Joy,
And Summer, with his fervid beaming eye:
All-cheering Plenty, with her flowing horn,
Led yellow Autumn, wreathed with nodding corn,
Then Winter's time-bleach'd locks did hoary show:
By Hospitality with cloudless brow.
Next follow'd Courage, with his martial stride,
From where the Feal wild-woody coverts hide;
Benevolence, with mild, benignant air,
A female form came from the towers of Stair:
Learning and Worth in equal measures trode
From simple Catrine, their long-loved abode;
Last, white-robed Peace, crowned with a hazel wreath,
To rustic Agriculture did bequeath
The broken iron instruments of death;
At sight of whom our sprites forgat their kindling wrath.

## ADDRESS OF BEELZEBUB
### TO THE PRESIDENT OF THE HIGHLAND SOCIETY.

#### ROBERT BURNS.

Long life, my lord, and health be yours
Unscaith'd by hunger'd Highland boors;
Lord, grant nae duddie desperate beggar,
Wi' dirk, claymore, or rusty trigger,

May twin auld Scotland o' a life
She likes—as lambkins like a knife.
Faith, you and A——s were right
To keep the Highland hounds in sight:
I doubt na! they wad bid nae better
Than let them ance out owre the water;
Then up amang the thae lakes and seas
They'll mak what rules and laws they please;
Some daring Hancock, or a Franklin,
May set their Highland bluid a ranklin';
Some Washington again may head them,
Or some Montgomery, fearless lead them,
Till God knows what may be effected
When by such heads and hearts directed—
Poor dunghill sons of dirt and mire
May to Patrician rights aspire!
Nae sage North, now, nor sager Sackville,
To watch and premier o'or the pack vile,
And whare will ye get Howes and Clintons
To bring them to a right repentance,
To cowe the rebel generation,
And save the honour o' the nation?
They and be damn'd! what right hae they
To meat or sleep, or light o' day?
Far less to riches, power, or freedom,
But what your lordship likes to gie them?

But hear, my lord! Glengarry, hear!
Your hand's owre light on them, I fear!
Your factors, grieves, trustees and bailies,
I canna say but they do gaylies;
Then lay aside a' tender mercies,
And tirl the hallions to the birses;
Yet while they're only poind't and herriet,
They'll keep their stubborn Highland spirit;
But smash them! crash them a' to spails!
And rot the dyvors i' the jails!
The young dogs, swinge them to the labor;
Let wark and hunger mak them sober!
The hizzies, if they're aughtlins fawsont,
Let them in Drury land be lesson'd

And if the wives and dirty brats
E'en thigger at your doors and yetts,
Flaffan wi' duds and gray wi' beas',
Frightin' awa' your ducks and geese,
Get out a horsewhip or a jowler,
The langest thong, the fiercest growler,
And gar the tatter'd gypsies pack
Wi' a' their bastards on their back !
Go on, my lord! I lang to meet you,
And in my house at hame to greet you;
Wi' common lords ye shanna mingle,
The benmost neuk beside the ingle,
At my right han' assign'd your seat,
"Tween Herod's hip and polycrate,—
Or if you on your station tarrow,
Between Almagro and Pizzaro,
A seat I'm sure ye're well deservin't;
And till ye come—Your humble servant,

BEELZEBUB.

---

## PROLOGUE,

SPOKEN BY MR. WOODS ON HIS BENEFIT NIGHT, APRIL 16, 1787.

### ROBERT BURNS.

WHEN by a generous public's kind acclaim,
That dearest meed is granted—honest fame,
When here your favor is the actor's lot,
Nor even the man in private life forgot;
What breast so dead to heavenly virtue's glow,
But heaves impassion'd with the grateful throe?

Poor is the task to please a barbarous throng,
It needs no Siddons' powers in Southern's song;
But here an ancient nation famed afar,
For genius, learning high, as great in war—
Hail, CALEDONIA ! name forever dear,
Before whose sons I'm honor'd to appear!
Where every science—every nobler art—
That can inform the mind, or mend the heart,

Is known: as grateful nations oft have found,
Far as the rude barbarian marks the bound.
Philosophy, no idle pedant dream,          [beam;
Here holds her search by heaven-taught reason's
Here History paints with elegance and force,
The tide of Empire's fluctuating course;
Here Douglas forms wild Shakespeare into plan,
And Harley rouses all the god in man,
When well-form'd taste and sparkling wit unite
With manly lore, or female beauty bright,
(Beauty, where faultless symmetry and grace,
Can only charm us in the second place),
Witness my heart, how oft with panting fear,
As on this night, I've met these judges here:
But still the hope Experience taught to live,
Equal to judge—you're candid to forgive.
No hundred-headed Riot here we meet,
With decency and law beneath his feet:
Nor insolence assumes fair Freedom's name;
Like CALEDONIANS, you applaud or blame.

O thou dread power! whose empire-giving hand
Has oft been stretch'd to shield the honour'd land!
Strong may she glow with all her ancient fire!
May every son be worthy of his sire !
Firm may she rise with generous disdain
At Tyranny's, or direr Pleasure's chain !
Still self-dependent in her native shore,
Bold may she brave grim Danger's loudest roar,
Till Fate the curtain drops on worlds to be no more.

## MAN WAS MADE TO MOURN.

ROBERT BURNS.

When chill November's surly blast
    Made fields and forests bare,
One evening, as I wander'd forth
    Along the banks of Ayr,
I spied a man whose aged step
    Seem'd weary worn with care;

His face was furrow'd o'er with years,
  And hoary was his hair.

"Young stranger, whither wanderest thou?"
  Began the reverend sage;
"Does thirst of wealth thy step constrain,
  Or youthful pleasures rage?
Or haply, prest with cares and woes,
  Too soon thou hast began
To wander forth with me to mourn
  The miseries of man.

"The sun that overhangs yon moors,
  Outspreading far and wide,
Where hundreds labour to support
  A haughty lordling's pride;
I've seen yon weary winter sun
  Twice forty times return,
And every time has added proofs
  That man was made to mourn.

"O man! while in thy early years,
  How prodigal of time!
Misspending all thy precious hours,
  Thy glorious youthful prime!
Alternate follies take the sway;
  Licentious passions burn;
Which tenfold force gives nature's law,
  That man was made to mourn.

"Look not alone on youthful prime,
  Or manhood's active might;
Man then is useful to his kind,
  Supported is his right,
But see him on the edge of life,
  With cares and sorrows worn;
Then age and want—oh! ill match'd pair!—
  Show man was made to mourn.

"A few seem favorites of fate,
  In pleasure's lap carest;
Yet think not all the rich and great

Are likewise truly blest.
But, oh! what crowds in every land
    Are wretched and forlorn !
Through weary life this lesson learn—
    That man was made to mourn.

"Many and sharp the numerous ills
    Inwoven with our fame !
More pointed still we make ourselves—
    Regret, remorse, and shame !
And man, whose heaven-erected face
    The smiles of love adorn,
Man's inhumanity to man
    Makes countless thousands mourn !

"See yonder poor, o'erlabor'd wight,
    So abject, mean and vile,
Who begs a brother of the earth
    To give him leave to toil;
And see his lordly fellow-worm
    The poor petition spurn,
Unmindful, though a weeping wife
    And helpless offspring mourn.

"If I'm design'd yon lordling's slave—
    By nature's law design'd—
Why was an independent wish
    E'er planted in my mind?
If not, why am I subject to
    His cruelty or scorn?
Or why has man the will and power
    To make his fellow mourn.

"Yet let not this too much, my son,
    Disturb thy youthful breast;
This partial view of human kind
    Is surely not the last !
The poor, oppress'd, honest man.
    Had never, sure, been born,
Had not there been some recompense
    To comfort those who mourn.

"O Death! the poor man's dearest friend—
  The kindest and the best!
Welcome the hour my aged limbs
  Are laid with thee at rest!
The great, the wealthy, fear thy blow,
  From pomp and pleasure torn;
But, oh! a blest relief to those
  That weary-laden mourn!"

## TO MARY IN HEAVEN.

### ROBERT BURNS.

Thou ling'ring star with less'ning ray,
  That lovest to greet the early morn,
Again thou usher'st in the day
  My Mary from my soul was torn.
O Mary! dear departed shade!
  Where is thy place of blissful rest?
See'st thou thy lover lowly laid?
  Hear'st thou the groans that rend his breast?

That sacred hour can I forget,
  Can I forget the hallow'd grove,
Where by the winding Ayr we met,
  To live one day of parting love!
Eternity will not efface
  Those records dear of transports past;
Thy image at our last embrace,
  Ah! little thought we 'twas our last!

Ayr, gurgling, kiss'd his pebbled shore,
  O'erhung with wildwoods thick'ning green,
The fragrant birch, and hawthorn hoar,
  Twined amorous round the raptured scene;
The flowers sprang wanton to be prest,
  The birds sang love on every spray—
Till too, too soon, the glowing west
  Proclaimed the speed of winged day.

Still o'er these scenes my memory wakes,

And fondly broods with miser care!
Time but the impression stronger makes,
  As streams their channels deeper wear.
My Mary! dear departed shade!
  Where is thy place of blissful rest!
See'st thou thy lover lowly laid?
  Hear'st thou the groans that rend his breast?

## BRUTUS' ADDRESS TO THE ROMANS.

### SHAKESPEARE.

Romans, countrymen, and lovers! hear me for my cause, and be silent, that you may hear: believe me for mine honor; and have respect to mine honor, that you may believe: censure me in your wisdom; and awake your senses, that you may the better judge. If there be any in this assembly, any dear friend of Cæsar's, to him I say, that Brutus' love to Cæsar was no less than his. If, then, that friend demand why Brutus rose against Cæsar, this is my answer,—not that I loved Cæsar less, but that I loved Rome more. Had you rather Cæsar were living and die all slaves, than that Cæsar were dead, to live all free men? As Cæsar loved me, I weep for him; as he was fortunate, I rejoice at it; as he was valiant, I honor him: but as he was ambitious, I slew him: There is tears for his love; joy for his fortune, honor for his valor; and death for his ambition. Who is here so base, that would be a bondman? If any, speak: for him have I offended. Who is here so rude, that would not be a Roman? If any, speak: for him have I offended. Who is here so vile, that will not love his country? If any, speak; for him have I offended. I pause for a reply.

*Citizens.* None, Brutus, none.

*Bru.* Then none have I offended. I have done no more to Cæsar, than you shall do to Brutus. The question of his death is enrolled in the Capitol: his glory not extenuated, wherein he was worthy; nor his offenses enforced, for which he suffered death.

*Enter* Antony *and others with* Cæsar's body.

Here comes his body, mourned by Mark Antony: who, though he had no hand in his death, shall receive the benefit of his dying, a place in the commonwealth; as which of you shall not? With this I depart,—that, as I slew my best lover for the good of Rome, I have the same dagger for myself, when it shall please my country to need my death.

## ANTONY'S ORATION AT CÆSAR'S FUNERAL.

### SHAKESPEARE.

Friends, Romans, countrymen, lend me your ears;
I come to bury Cæsar, not to praise him.
The evil that men do lives after them;
The good is oft interred with their bones;
So let it be with Cæsar. The noble Brutus
Hath told you Cæsar was ambitious:
If it were so, it was a grievous fault;
And grievously hath Cæsar answered it.
Here, under leave of Brutus and the rest,
(For Brutus is an honorable man;
So are they all, all honorable men,)
Come I to speak in Cæsar's funeral.
He was my friend, faithful and just to me:
But Brutus says he was ambitious;
And Brutus is an honorable man.
He hath brought many captives home to Rome,
Whose ransoms did the general coffers fill:
Did this in Cæsar seem ambitious?
When that the poor hath cried, Cæsar hath wept:
Ambition should be made of sterner stuff:
Yet Brutus says he was ambitious;
And Brutus is an honorable man.
You all did see that on the Lupercal
I thrice presented him a kingly crown,
Which he did thrice refuse: was this ambition?
Yet Brutus says he was ambitious;
And, sure, he is an honorable man.
I speak not to disprove what Brutus spoke,
But here I am to speak what I do know.
You all did love him once, not without cause:
What cause withholds you, then, to mourn for him?
O judgment, thou art fled to brutish beasts,

And men have lost their reason!—Bear with me;
My heart is in the coffin there with Cæsar,
And I must pause till it come back to me.
   But yesterday, the word of Cæsar might
Have stood against the world: now, lies he there,
And none so poor to do him reverence.
O masters! if I were dispos'd to stir
Your hearts and minds to mutiny and rage,
I should do Brutus wrong, and Cassius wrong,
Who, you all know, are honorable men:
I will not do them wrong; I rather choose
To wrong the dead, to wrong myself, and you,
Than I will wrong such honorable men.
But here's a parchment with the seal of Cæsar,
I found it in his closet; 'tis his will:
Let but the commons hear this testament,
(Which, pardon me, I do not mean to read,)
And they would go and kiss dead Cæsar's wounds,
And dip their napkins in his sacred blood;
Yea, beg a hair of him for memory,
And, dying, mention it within their wills,
Bequeathing it as a rich legacy
Unto their issue.
   *Citizens.*   The will, the will! we will hear Cæsar's will.
   *Ant.*   Have patience, gentle friends, I must not read it;
It is not meet you know how Cæsar loved you.
You are not wood, you are not stones, but men;
And, being men, hearing the will of Cæsar,
It will inflame you, it will make you mad:
'Tis good you know not that you are his heirs;
For if you should, O, what would come of it!
   *4 Cit.*   Read the will, we'll hear it Antony;
   *Ant.*   You will compel me, then, to read the will?
Then make a ring about the corse of Cæsar,
And let me show you him that made the will.
Shall I descend? and will you give leave?
   *Citizens.*   Stand back; room: bear back.
   *Ant.*   If you have tears, prepare to shed them now.
You all do know this mantle: I remember
The first time ever Cæsar put it on;
'Twas on a summer's evening in his tent,

That day he overcame the Nervii:—
Look, in this place, ran Cassius' dagger through:
See what a rent the envious Casca made:
Through this the well-beloved Brutus stabb'd,
And, as he plucked his cursed steel away,
Mark how the blood of Cæsar follow'd it,
As rushing out of doors, to be resolv'd
If Brutus so unkindly knock'd, or no;
For Brutus, as you know, was Cæsar's angel:
Judge, O you gods, how dearly Cæsar lov'd him.
This was the most unkindest cut of all;
For when the noble Cæsar saw him stab,
Ingratitude, more strong than traitor's arms,
Quite vanquish'd him: then burst his mighty heart,
And, in his mantle muffling up his face,
Even at the base of Pompey's statue,
Which all the while ran blood, great Cæsar fell.
O, what a fall was there, my countrymen!
Then I, and you, and all of us fell down,
Whilst bloody treason flourish'd over us.
O, now you weep; and, I perceive you feel
The dint of pity: these are gracious drops.
Kind souls, what, weep you when you but behold
Our Cæsar's vesture wounded? Look you here,
Here is himself, marr'd, as you see, with traitors.

Good friends, sweet friends, let me not stir you up
To such a sudden flood of mutiny.
They that have done this deed, are honorable:
What private griefs they have, alas, I know not,
That made them do it; they are wise and honorable,
And will, no doubt with reasons answer you.
I come not, friends, to steal away your hearts;
I am no orator, as Brutus is:
But, as you know me all, a plain blunt man,
That love my friend; and that they know full well,
That gave me public leave to speak of him.
For I have neither wit, nor words, nor worth,
Action, nor utterance, nor the power of speech,
To stir men's blood: I only speak right on;
I tell you that, which yourselves do know:

Show you sweet Cæsar's wounds, poor, poor dumb mouths,
And bid them speak for me: But were I Brutus,
And Brutus Antony, there were an Antony
Would ruffle up your spirits, and put a tongue
In every wound of Cæsar, that should move
The stones of Rome to rise and mutiny.

---

# HAMLET'S ADVICE TO THE PLAYERS.

SHAKESPEARE.

Speak the speech, I pray you, as I pronounced it to you, trippingly on the tongue: but if you mouth it, as many of our players do, I had as lief the town-crier spoke my lines. Nor do not saw the air too much with your hand, thus, but use all gently: for in the very torrent, tempest, and as I may say, whirlwind of your passion, you must acquire and beget a temperance, that may give it smoothness. O, it offends me to the soul, to hear a robustuous periwig-pated fellow tear a passion to tatters, to very rags, to split the ears of the groundlings, who, for the most part, are capable of nothing but inexplicable dumb show and noise: I would have such a fellow whipt for o'er-doing Termagant; it out-herods Herod: pray you avoid it.

Be not too tame neither, but let your own discretion be your tutor: suit the action to the word, the word to the action: with this special observance, that you o'erstep not the modesty of nature: for anything so overdone is from the purpose of playing; whose end both at first, and now, was and is to hold, as 'twere, the mirror up to nature; to show virtue her own feature, scorn her own image, and the very age and body of the time, his form and pressure. Now this, overdone, or come tardy off, though it make the unskillful laugh, cannot but make the judicious grieve; the censure of which one, must in your allowance, o'erweigh a whole theater of others. O, there be players, that I have seen play, and heard others praise, and that highly, not to speak it profanely, that, neither having the accent of Christians, nor the gait of Christian, pagan, nor man, have so strutted and bellowed, that I have thought some of nature's journeymen had made them, and not made them well, they imitated humanity so abominably.

## HAMLET'S SOLILOQUY ON DEATH.

**SHAKESPEARE.**

To be or not to be,—that is the question;
Whether 'tis nobler in the mind to suffer
The slings and arrows of outrageous fortune,
Or to take arms against a sea of troubles,
And by opposing end them? To die,—to sleep:—
No more; and, by a sleep, to say we end
The heart ache, and the thousand natural shocks
That flesh is heir to,—'tis a consumation
Devoutly to be wished. To die,—to sleep;—
To sleep! perchance to dream:—ay, there's the rub,
For in that sleep of death what dreams may come,
When we have shuffled off this mortal coil,
Must give us pause: there's the respect
That makes calamity of so long life;
For who would bear the whips and scorns of time,
The oppressor's wrong, the proud man's contumely,
The pangs of despis'd love, the law's delay,
The insolence of office, and the spurns
That patient merit of the unworthy takes,
When he himself might his quietus make
With a bare bodkin? who would fardels bear,
To grunt and sweat under a weary life,
But that the dread of something after death,
The undiscover'd country, from whose bourn
No traveler returns, puzzles the will,
And makes us rather bear those ills we have,
Than fly to others that we know not of?
Thus conscience does make cowards of us all;
And thus the native hue of resolution
Is sicklied o'er with the pale cast of thought;
And enterprises of great pith and moment,
With this regard, their currents turn awry,
And lose the name of action.

We wouldn't ask no better fun than jist to make him climb;
We'd hev a long vacation an' a whooper of a time.

The teacher he wuz sickly—he wuz not ez big ez I—
I knew that we could bounce him if we didn't but half try,
Fur any one lookin' at him would a' said on sight
Ther' wuzn't eny sand in him an' not a speck o' fight.
His hands they wa'n't accustomed much to hangin' on to ploughs,
To hoein' corn, to cradlin' wheat, or milkin' twenty cows;
Philetus said he'd use him for a mop to mop the floor,
An' when he begged an' hollered that we'd h'ist him out the door.

I 'e told the boys at recess o' the plot we had planned;
They said 'f we couldn't down him they'd lend a helpin' hand;
But big Philetus Phinney, he wuz tickled ez could be
To think that they tho't a snip like that could lick a chap like he;
'F I'd kick the bucket over, he'd make the teacher dance—
He'd flop him in the water, he'd mop it with his pants.

We heard the school bell ringin', we scrambled in pell-mell;
I run ag'in' the water-pail, on puppus, an' I fell;
I struck upon a stick o' wood, I badly raked my shin,
The water swoshed upon me, an' it wet me to the skin.

The scrawny little teacher, why! he bounded from his chair,
He took me by the trousers, and he held me in the air,
Then round an' round an' round an' round he whirled me like a top,
An' when I seed a thousand stars he suddenly let me drop;
He took me an' he shook me till I tho't that I should die,
He swished me with his ruler till my pants were nearly dry,
While big Philetus Phinney he wuz just too scar'd to laugh,
He let the teacher lick me till I bellowed like a calf.

An' all the other fightin' boys, with white an' frightened looks,
Sot shakin' in the'r very boots an' ras'lin with the'r books;
An' oh, how hard they studied—not a feller spoke or stirred—
They didn't dar' to whisper or to say a single word.
Whar' is that little teacher that giv' me such a scar'?
He still is peaked lookin'—he's setten' over thar'—
An' tho' he's nearly seventy, an' sickly yit, I vow
I'd hate to hev him git those hands o' his'n on me now.
He taught me one great lesson by that floggin' in his school;
That a braggart an' a bully ar' a coward an' a fool.

# BINGEN ON THE RHINE.

### CAROLINE E. NORTON.

A soldier of the Legion lay dying in Algiers:
There was lack of woman's nursing, there was dearth of woman's tears;
But a comrade stood beside him, while his life-blood ebbed away,
And bent with pitying glances, to hear what he might say.
The dying soldier faltered, as he took that comrade's hand,
And he said, "I never more shall see my own, my native land.
Take a message and a token to some distant friends of mine;
For I was born at Bingen—at Bingen on the Rhine!

"Tell my brothers and companions, when they meet and crowd around,
To hear my mournful story, in the pleasant vineyard ground,
That we fought the battle bravely; and when the day was done,
Full many a corpse lay ghastly pale beneath the setting sun.
And midst the dead and dying were some grown old in wars,
The death-wounds on their gallant breasts the last of many scars;
But some were young, and suddenly beheld life's morn decline;
And one had come from Bingen—fair Bingen on the Rhine!

"Tell my mother that her other sons shall comfort her old age,
For I was still a truant bird that thought his home a cage;
For my father was a soldier, and even as a child
My heart leaped forth to hear him tell of struggles fierce and wild;
And when he died, and left us to divide his scanty hoard,
I let them take whate'er they would—but kept my father's sword;
And with boyish love I hung it, where the bright light used to shine
On the cottage wall at Bingen—calm Bingen on the Rhine!

"Tell my sister not to weep for me, and sob with drooping head,
When the troops come marching home again, with glad and gallant tread;
But to look upon them proudly, with a calm and steadfast eye,
For her brother was a soldier, too, and not afraid to die;
And if a comrade seek her love, I ask her in my name
To listen to him kindly, without regret or shame;
And to hang the old sword in its place, my father's sword and mine,
For the honor of old Bingen—dear Bingen on the Rhine!

" There's another, not a sister; in the happy days gone by
You'd have known her by the merriment that sparkled in her eye;

Too innocent for coquetry, too fond for idle scorning;
O friend! I fear the lightest heart makes sometimes heaviest mourning.
Tell her the last night night of my life (for ere this moon be risen,
My body will be out of pain, my soul be out of prison,)
I dreamed I stood with her, and saw the yellow sunlight shine
On the vine-clad hills of Bingen—fair Bingen on the Rhine!

"I saw the blue Rhine sweep along; I heard, or seemed to hear,
The German songs we used to sing, in chorus sweet and clear;
And down the pleasant river, and up the slanting hill,
The echoing chorus sounded, through the evening calm and still;
And her glad blue eyes were on me, as we passed, with friendly talk,
Down many a path beloved of yore, and well-remembered walk;
And her little hand lay lightly, confidingly in mine:
But we'll meet no more at Bingen—loved Bingen on the Rhine!"

His voice grew faint and hoarse—his grasp was childish weak;
His eyes put on a dying look—he sighed, and ceased to speak;
His comrade bent to lift him, but the spark of life had fled:
The soldier of the legion in a foreign land was dead!
And the soft moon rose up slowly, and calmly she looked down
On the red sand of the battlefield, with bloody corpses strown.
Yes, calmly on that dreadful scene her pale light seemed to shine,
As it shown on distant Bingen—fair Bingen on the Rhine!

---

## MARION.

WILLIAM CULLEN BRYANT.

Our band is few, but true and tried,
 Our leader frank and bold;
The British soldier trembles
When Marion's name is told.
Our fortress is the good greenwood,
 Our tent the cypress-tree;
We know the forest round us,
 As seamen know the sea;
We know its walls of thorny vines,
 Its glades of reedy grass,
Its safe and silent islands
 Within the dark morass.

Woe to the English soldiery
  That little dread us near!
On them shall light at midnight
  A strange and sudden fear;
When, waking to their tents on fire,
  They grasp their arms in vain,
And they who stand to face us
  Are beat to earth again;
And they who fly in terror deem
  A mighty host behind,
And hear the tramp of thousands
  Upon the hollow wind.

Then sweet the hour that brings release
  From danger and from toil;
We talk the battle over,
  And share the battle's spoil.
The woodland rings with laugh and shout,
  As if a hunt were up,
And woodland flowers are gathered
  To crown the soldier's cup.
With merry songs we mock the wind
  That in the pine-top grieves,
And slumber long and sweetly
  On beds of oaken leaves.

Well knows the fair and friendly moon
  The band that Marion leads,—
The glitter of their rifles,
  The scampering of their steeds.
'T is life to guide the fiery barb
  Across the moonlight plain;
'T is life to feel the night-wind
  That lifts his tossing mane.
A moment in the British camp—
  A moment—and away
Back to the pathless forest,
  Before the peep of day.

Grave men there are by the broad Santee,
  Grave men with hoary hairs;
Their hearts are all with Marion,

For Marion are their prayers.
And lovely ladies greet our band
  With kindliest welcoming,
  With smiles like those of summer,
  And tears like those of spring.
For them we wear these trusty arms,
  And lay them down no more
Till we have driven the Briton
  Forever from our shore.

## LITTLE BREECHES.

A PIKE COUNTY VIEW OF SPECIAL PROVIDENCE.

JOHN HAY.

I don't go much on religion,
  I never ain't had no show;
But I've got a middlin' tight grip, sir,
  On the handful o' things I know.
I don't pan out on the prophets
  And free-will, and that sort of thing,—
But I b'lieve in God and the angels,
  Ever sence one night last spring.

I come into town with some turnips,
  And my little Gabe come along,—
No four-year-old in the county
  Could beat him for pretty and strong,
Peart and chipper and sassy,
  Always ready to swear and to fight,—
And I'd larnt him ter chaw terbacker,
  Jest to keep his milk-teeth white.

The snow come down like a blanket
  As I passed by Taggart's store;
I went in for a jug of molasses
  And left the team at the door.
They scared at something and started,—
  I heard one little squall,
And hell-to-split over the prairie
  Went team, Little Breeches and all.

Hell-to-split over the prairie !
  I was almost froze with skeer;
But we rousted up some torches,
  And sarched for 'em far and near.
At last we struck hosses and wagon,
  Snowed under a soft white mound,
Upsot, dead beat,—but of little Gabe
  No hide nor hair was found.

And here all hope soured on me
  Of my fellow-critter's aid,—
I jest flopped down on my marrow-bones,
  Crotch-deep in the snow, and prayed.

  \*    \*    \*    \*    \*

By this, the torches was played out,
  And me and Isrul Parr
Went off for some wood to a sheepfold
  That he said was somewhar thar.

We found it at last, and a little shed
  Where they shut up the lambs at night.
We looked in, and seen them huddled thar,
  So warm and sleepy and white;
And THAR sot Little Breeches and chirped,
  As peart as ever you see,
"I want a chaw of terbacker,
  And that's what's the matter of me."

How did he get thar? Angels.
  He could never have walked in that storm.
They jest scooped down and toted him
  To whar it was safe and warm.
And I think that saving a little child,
  And bringing him to his own,
Is a derned sight better business
  Than loafing around The Throne.

## THE BLACKSMITH'S STORY.

### FRANK OLIVE.

Well, no; my wife ain't dead, sir,
    But I've lost her all the same;
She left me voluntarily,
    And neither was to blame.
It's rather a queer story,
    And I think you will agree,
When you hear the circumstances,
    'Twas rather rough on me.

She was a soldier's widow,
    He was killed at Malvern Hill;
And when I married her she seemed
    To sorrow for him still;
But I brought her here to Kansas,
    And I never want to see
A better wife than Mary was
    For five bright years to me.

The change of scene brought cheerfulness,
    And soon a rosy glow
Of happiness warmed Mary's cheeks
    And melted all their snow.
I think she loved me some—I'm bound
    To think that of her, sir,
And as for me—I can't begin
    To tell how I loved her!

Three year ago the baby came
    Our humble home to bless,
And then I reckon I was nigh
    To perfect happiness;
'Twas hers—'twas mine; but no language
    Have I to explain to you
How that little girl's weak fingers
    Our hearts together drew.

Once we watched it through a fever,
    And with each gasping breath,
Dumb with an awful wordless woe,
    We waited for its death:
And, though I'm not a pious man,

Our souls together there,
  For Heaven to spare our darling
Went up in voiceless prayer.

And when the doctor said 'twould live,
  Our joy what words could tell?
Clasped in each other's arms we stood,
  And our grateful tears fell,
Sometimes, you see, the shadows fell
  Across our little nest,
But it only made the sunshine seem
  A doubly welcome guest.

Work came to me a plenty,
  And I kept the anvil ringing—
Early and late you'd find me there,
  A-hammering and singing;
Love nerved my arm to labor,
  And moved my tongue to song,
And though my singing wasn't sweet,
  It was tremendous strong.

One day a one-armed stranger stopped
  To have me nail a shoe,
And while I was at work we passed
  A compliment or two;
I asked him how he lost his arm.
    He said 'twas shot away
At Malvern Hill. "At Malvern Hill!
  Did you know Robert May?"

"That's me," said he. "You, you!" I gasped,
  Choking with horrid doubt;
"If you're the man, just follow me;
  We'll try this mystery out!"
With dizzy steps I led him to
  My Mary. God! God! 'twas true!
Then the bitterest pangs of misery
  Unspeakable I knew.

Frozen with deadly horror,
  She stared with eyes of stone,
And from her quivering lips there broke
  One wild despairing moan.

'Twas he! the husband of her youth,
  Now risen from the dead.
But all too late—and with bitter cry,
  Reeling, her senses fled.

What could be done?  He was believed
  As dead.  On his return
He strove in vain some tidings
  Of his absent wife to learn.
'Twas well that he was innocent,
  Else I'd have killed him, too,
So dead he never would have riz
  Till Gabriel's trumpet blew!

It was agreed that Mary then
  Between us should decide,
And each by her decision
  Would sacredly abide.
No sinner at the judgment-seat,
  Waiting eternal doom,
Could suffer what I then did,
  Waiting sentence in that room.

Rigid and breathless there we stood,
  With nerves as tense as steel,
While Mary's eyes sought each white face
  In piteous appeal.
God! could not woman's duty
  Be less hardly reconciled
Between her lawful husband
  And the father of her child?

Ah! how my heart was chilled to ice,
  When she knelt down and said:
" Forgive me, John!  'Tis my husband
  Here—alive, not dead!"
I raised her tenderly, and tried
  To tell her she was right,
But somehow in my aching breast
  The prisoned words stuck tight.

" But, John, I can't leave baby!"
  " What! wife and child?" cried I;
" Must I yield all?  Ah, cruel fate!

Better that I should die.
Think of the long, sad, lonely hours
  Waiting in gloom for me—
No wife to cheer me with her love,
  No babe to climb my knee!

"And yet you are her mother,
  And the sacred mother love
Is still the purest, tenderest tie
  That Heaven ever wove.
Take her—but promise, Mary—
  For that will bring no shame—
My little girl shall bear and learn
  To lisp her father's name!"

It may be, in the life to come,
  I'll meet my child and wife;
But yonder, by my cottage gate,
  We parted for this life;
One long hand clasp from Mary,
  And my dream of love was done—
One long embrace from baby,
  And my happiness was gone.

# INDEX.

www.ingramcontent.com/pod-product-compliance
Lightning Source LLC
Chambersburg PA
CBHW031243260626
47169CB00007B/2430